Jpb Easy G

This book is a work of fiction. Any references to historical events, real people, or real places are used fictitiously. Other names, characters, places, and events are products of the author's imagination, and any resemblance to actual events or places or persons, living or dead, is entirely coincidental.

LITTLE SIMON

An imprint of Simon & Schuster Children's Publishing Division • 1230 Avenue of the Americas, New York, New York 10020 • First Little Simon paperback edition October 2015. Copyright © 2015 by Simon & Schuster, Inc. All rights reserved, including the right of reproduction in whole or in part in any form. LITTLE SIMON is a registered trademark of Simon & Schuster, Inc., and associated colophon is a trademark of Simon & Schuster, Inc. For information about special discounts for bulk purchases, please contact Simon & Schuster Special Sales at 1-866-506-1949 or business@simonandschuster.com. The Simon & Schuster Speakers Bureau can bring authors to your live event. For more information or to book an event contact the Simon & Schuster Speakers Bureau at 1-866-248-3049 or visit our website at www.simonspeakers.com.
Designed by Laura Roode. The text of this book was set in Usherwood.
Manufactured in the United States of America 0915 FFG
10 9 8 7 6 5 4 3 2 1
Cataloging-in-Publication Data for this title is
available from the Library of Congress.
ISBN 978-1-4814-4197-1 (hc)
ISBN 978-1-4814-4196-4 (pbk)
ISBN 978-1-4814-4198-8 (eBook)

the adventures of

SOPHIE MOUSE

5

The Maple Festival

By Poppy Green • Illustrated by Jennifer A. Bell

LITTLE SIMON

New York London Toronto Sydney New Delhi

Contents

Lily Mouse had 100 maple tarts to sell at the maple festival. She sold 20 before lunch. She sold 10 after lunch. How many did she have left to take home to her family?

Fall Fun

Sophie Mouse tapped her pencil on her school desk. Her assignment was to write a math word problem. Sophie wondered if Mrs. Wise would like hers.

Mmmm . . . thought Sophie as she reread the problem. Autumn was a very yummy time of year. It was when her mom made all kinds of maple treats at her bakery in Pine Needle Grove. And every year, Mrs. Mouse sold them at the big Maple Festival. Sophie couldn't wait for this year's festival. It was coming up this weekend!

A cool breeze blew in through the window. It carried a few leaves with it.

"Okay, class!" Mrs. Wise called out. "Time for recess!"

The whole class jumped up. Sophie joined her friends Hattie Frog and Owen Snake at the door. They headed out to the playground.

"Are you both going to the Maple Festival this weekend?" Sophie asked them.

Hattie nodded. "Of course!" she said. "I want to ride the Ferris wheel at least five times!"

Owen gasped. "There will be a Ferris wheel?" His family had moved to Pine Needle Grove a few months before. He had never been to the Maple Festival.

"Owen, there's so much to do there!" Sophie cried. The three friends were nearing the swings. "There's dragonfly racing. You can play games to win prizes, like cranberry necklaces and acorn-top yo-yos!"

"There are ribbon-dancing grasshoppers!" added Zoe, a bluebird who was swinging on a swing.

"And my mom's bake stand too!" added Winston, Sophie's little brother. He ran between Sophie and Hattie and was gone in a flash.

"Yummm," said several students, rubbing their bellies. Lily Mouse's bake stand was always one of the most popular attractions at the festival.

Ben, a rabbit who was Sophie's age, called out from the top of the slide. "I heard there's going to be a fire-breathing lizard this year!"

Sophie, Hattie, Owen, and Zoe looked at him in surprise.

Ben shrugged. "What?" he said. "That's what I heard!"

At home that evening, Sophie's mom and dad were talking about the festival too. "It's going to be a busy week," George Mouse said. He was an architect. Every year, he helped animals build their festival stands.

Lily Mouse looked more tired than usual. She had worked all day at the bakery. "Mrs. Fields isn't going to be able to help me this year. She is visiting friends in Briar Patch."

A chipmunk named Mrs. Fields usually helped Lily Mouse the week before the festival. There was so much extra baking to do.

Sophie hurried over to her mom. "I can help you!" she offered. "I could be your assistant!"

Lily Mouse smoothed the fur on Sophie's head. "Thank you, Sophie," she said. "But I think I might need a grown-up to help me."

Sophie clasped her hands together. "Oh pleeeease, Mom," she pleaded.

"You've always said that I'm a big help in the kitchen."

Lily Mouse looked at Sophie. She seemed to be thinking it over.

Finally, she said, "Okay. We'll give it a try. You can start after school tomorrow."

Sophie cheered. Her mom smiled, but held up a hand.

"But don't say I didn't warn you," said Mrs. Mouse "There's a *lot* to do!"

chapter 2

Delicious
Daydreams

After school the next day, Sophie dropped Winston off at his friend James's house for a playdate. Then Sophie hurried toward the bakery. She was excited to be her mom's assistant for the Maple Festival!

Sophie ran through the village of Pine Needle Grove. Her nose picked up the sweet scent of maple sugar.

Minutes later, she arrived at the bakery. She opened the front door.

"Hello?" Sophie called. There was no one up front.

Suddenly, there was a loud clatter from the kitchen. Sophie followed the sound. She pushed open the kitchen door. Her mom was standing in the middle of the room. At her feet was an overturned bowl and a puddle of batter.

"Oh dear," Lily Mouse cried. "I worked for *hours* on that maple cupcake batter." Her mom sighed.

Sophie patted her mom on the

back. "I'll help you clean it up," she said. "Then we can mix up another batch."

Lily Mouse looked up at Sophie and smiled. "Thank you, sweetie," she said. "I've been rushing about all day. And I'm trying to come up with some new recipes for this year's festival. But I haven't thought of anything yet."

Sophie grabbed a mop. As she cleaned up the batter, she wondered if *she* could come up with a new recipe. *What would I invent if I were a baker?* Sophie thought. *What tastes good with maple?*

Daffodil petal? No. Too bitter. Pine cone dust? Nah. Too spicy. Then Sophie stopped mopping. She had an idea!

"Mom," Sophie said, "how about a recipe that combines maple and apple?" Sophie thought it sounded perfect for autumn!

Lily Mouse was at the sink, washing the mixing bowl. She stopped scrubbing. A smile slowly lit up her face.

"Now why didn't I think of that?"
Lily Mouse said. "What a wonderful
idea, Sophie!"

chapter 3

Miss Olsen's orchard

Lily Mouse was out of apples. So she and Sophie each grabbed an empty basket. They walked together to the apple orchard. It was near Goldmoss Pond, not too far from the bakery.

"Hello!" Miss Olsen, a small gray squirrel, called to them as they walked up. Her family had run the orchard for years. "What can I get you today, Mrs. Mouse?"

Sophie loved coming to Olsen Orchard. There were so many different kinds of apples! There were small red ones that the small animals liked. There were large green ones for the bigger animals. And there were lots of sizes in between in red, yellow, green, and even pink.

At Olsen Orchard, you could pick your own apples. Or the squirrels could pick them for you. They worked in pairs. One squirrel scurried up a tree in a flash. She picked an apple and dropped it down to another squirrel, who caught it in a basket.

Lily Mouse told Miss Olsen that she needed lots of different kinds of apples. "My *assistant,* Sophie, and I are making some maple-apple treats

for the festival!" Sophie stood up straight. She felt proud to be introduced that way.

Miss Olsen smiled at Sophie. "Do you want to help pick the apples?"

Sophie beamed.

"Sure!" she exclaimed.

Miss Olsen called over two other squirrels. They started picking apples from the taller trees. Sophie got started on a shorter tree with yellow apples on it. She climbed up to the highest branch. She reached

out to an apple on the end. Then she twisted it while pulling gently and— *pluck!* One perfect apple!

Before long, Sophie had filled about half her basket. She looked

over at the squirrels. Their basket
was completely overflowing!

"I think that's plenty!" Lily Mouse
called out. She thanked Miss Olsen.
But when she and Sophie tried to

pick up the baskets, they were too heavy to carry.

So Miss Olsen loaded the baskets into her wheelbarrow. Then she walked Sophie and her mom back to the bakery.

"You must be very busy this week too!" Lily Mouse said to Miss Olsen. Olsen Orchard always had a stand at the festival.

"Will you be in charge of the apple carving again?" Sophie asked.

Miss Olsen nodded. "Yes! And this year the organizers asked us to create a huge apple sculpture as well. It

will be on display right next to the Ferris wheel!"

Wow! thought Sophie. *This really is going to be the biggest and best festival yet!*

chapter 4

Lots of Leaves

At school the next day, Sophie was daydreaming at her desk. She thought she could still smell the maple-apple muffins she and her mom had made the day before.

Sophie stared out the window. She made a list of her recipe ideas in her head.

Fluffy orange-and-clove cakes.

Poppy-seed doughnuts. Cranberry-nut cookies. And we'll need more maple treats. Maybe maple-glazed waffles? Two of them, with a layer of whipped cream in between! Sophie's mouth began to water.

"Sophie!" a voice whispered. Sophie shook herself out of her delicious daydream. "Sophie, Mrs. Wise is waiting for you!"

It was Hattie, standing at Sophie's side. Sophie looked around. The rest of the class was lined up at the schoolhouse door. Everyone's eyes were on Sophie.

"Well, Sophie?" Mrs. Wise said. "Are you going to join us on our leaf walk?"

Sophie jumped up and hurried to the end of the line. "Sorry!" she said. "I was just . . . thinking about something."

Mrs. Wise smiled and led the class

outside. She took the class on a leaf
walk every autumn. They identified
trees by their leaves. They pointed
out the brightest ones. And each stu-
dent collected a few fallen leaves.
Back at school, they would use them
to make leaf rubbings.

Mrs. Wise led the class out of

the schoolyard. They turned down a looping path through some dense woods.

Here they were free to stop and collect their leaves.

"I found birch!" called out Lydie, Hattie's sister. She held up a yellow leaf.

"Here's an elm!" shouted Owen, pointing with his tail.

Winston held up a brown leaf. "Oak!" he

called out. Sophie smiled. She and Winston both knew oak leaves very well. Their house was at the base of an oak tree.

Sophie scanned the ground as they walked on. She was looking for one certain type of leaf. . . .

She scurried toward a pile of bright red leaves under a large tree. She picked one up. "Maple!" Sophie announced.

Mrs. Wise nodded. "That's right!" she said. "Maple seems to be on *everyone's* mind this week!"

Mrs. Wise led the class back to the school. They spent their art time making their leaf rubbings. Sophie's was a rubbing of three maple leaves.

At recess, the whole class made a huge leaf pile in the middle of the playground. Then they lined up to take turns jumping in it.

Sophie took a running leap and

disappeared into the pile. The leaves were so soft! Sophie popped out of the pile, a huge grin on her face. "Autumn is awesome!" she exclaimed.

chapter 5

Ready, Set, Bake!

Sophie hurried to the bakery after school. She had written down all of her ideas on a page in her sketchbook.

"I love them!" Lily Mouse cried when she read them. "I love them all." She stood up and tossed Sophie an apron. "I guess we better get busy!"

So that afternoon, Sophie and her mom made orange-and-clove cakes,

poppy-seed doughnuts, and cran-berry nut cookies.

Lily Mouse gave Sophie baking tips as they worked.

"Measure carefully!" said Lily Mouse as they mixed the cake bat-ter. "A teaspoon of baking powder is usually plenty. A *tablespoon* is usu-ally . . . a *disaster.*"

She showed Sophie how to glaze the donuts while they were still warm. "If they are too cool, the glaze won't stick," said Lily Mouse.

She let Sophie mix the cookie

batter all by herself. "Don't overmix," said Lily Mouse. "Stir just until all of the ingredients are combined. Then the cookies will be soft and chewy."

The next day, they made dozens of waffle-cream sandwiches. "How did you come up with this idea, Sophie?" asked Lily Mouse.

Sophie smiled and shrugged. "It just came to me at school yesterday."

Lily Mouse smiled. "Hmmm," she said. "Daydreaming at school, are we?"

Sophie's whiskers twitched, but

she didn't say anything.

The day before the festival, they made lots of Lily Mouse's tried-and-true recipes.

They made pecan custard and pumpkin pies.

They made carrot cupcakes and apple-berry tarts.

Last but not least, they made giant maple cookies. They rolled

out the dough and cut each one in the shape of a maple leaf.

When the cookies came out of the oven, Sophie got to decorate them with icing. She made each one a little bit different.

At the end of the day, Sophie and
her mom looked around the bakery
kitchen.

The countertop was crowded with

trays and baskets full of muffins, cookies, scones, breads, and waffle-cream sandwiches.

The catering cart was piled high

with the first load of cakes and pies. They would take it over to the festival grounds early the next morning.

"Do you think we made enough?" asked Sophie.

"Well," said Lily Mouse, "everyone says there will be more animals at the festival than ever before. Let's hope we can feed them all!"

Lily Mouse turned off the kitchen light. Then she and Sophie went out the back door of the bakery. They headed home to the oak tree to rest up for the big day.

chapter 6

All Work, No Play

"Well, this is it!" said George Mouse. He lifted the last pie off the catering cart.

The whole family—Mr. Mouse, Mrs. Mouse, Sophie, and Winston— had worked together to get all the baked goods from the bakery to the festival grounds. They had started before sunrise that morning. It had taken many trips back and forth.

Now, finally, the bake stand was stocked and ready.

"Just in time," said Sophie. "Look!" A few animals were strolling into the festival.

For the first time that morning, Sophie had a chance to look around. Colorful flags flapped atop the tents. Musicians were warming up their instruments. The scent of popcorn and other festival foods filled the air. And, off in the distance, Sophie thought she caught a glimpse of the Olsens' apple sculpture. She hoped

to get a closer look later.

Sophie glanced up. Towering over everything was the giant Ferris wheel!

In the middle of it all was Lily Mouse's bake stand—one stand in a long row of many other stands. Each

one had crafts, or food for sale, or
games to play.

Lily Mouse looked up and down
the row. "There are definitely more
stands this year," she pointed out. "I
hope customers can find us!"

"Don't worry, Mom," Sophie said. "Animals come from far and wide to taste your treats, remember?"

Mr. Mouse took Winston by the hand. "Hey, Winston!" he said, looking around excitedly. "How about

you and I go check out the games?"

They headed off, leaving Sophie and her mom to wait for their first customers.

A few minutes later, Sophie saw Hattie, Lydie, and their parents walking toward them.

"My goodness!" exclaimed Mrs. Frog. "I heard the festival would be bigger than ever.

But this is really something!"

"Everything looks delicious!" said Mr. Frog.

Sophie grabbed Hattie by the

hand. "Let me show you some of the things *I* made."

Sophie showed Hattie the maple cookies she'd decorated. Suddenly, she felt a tap on her back. She turned around.

"Owen!" cried Sophie.

Owen's eyes were wide in amazement. "There's so much to see here!" he said. "I don't know where to start!"

Hattie looked at Sophie. "Let's

go find all the cool new stuff we heard about!"

"Yes!" Sophie cried. She looked over at her mom to tell her—then stopped. She couldn't just run off. That wasn't what a good assistant would do.

Sophie's heart sank. She had been so excited to help out at the festival. But she hadn't realized what it meant.

If she was helping the whole time, she wouldn't be able to have *fun*, too.

chapter 7

The Best
Festival Ever!

Suddenly, Mrs. Mouse came over to them. "Sophie, why don't you go explore the festival with Hattie and Owen?" she suggested. "You've earned it after all your hard work this week!"

Sophie gave her mom a hug. "Thank you!" she said. "I'll be back later when your line gets long!"

Sophie grabbed her satchel. Inside,
as usual, were her art supplies. She
carried them in case she saw something she just *had* to draw. She slung
the satchel over her shoulder and ran
off with her friends.

They zipped from stand to stand. They watched some animals playing a new game called tree-stump ring toss. One chipmunk tossed three rings over a tree stump and won! His prize was a big, shiny balloon.

They'd never had balloons at the festival before!

The friends stopped to check out a giant spider's web that was so strong animals could climb up it! The spider stood proudly in front of it, encouraging the animals to try.

Sophie, Hattie, and Owen passed a hopping panda . . . then realized it was Willy, a toad from school, wearing face paint.

"Willy! That looks so real!" cried Sophie.

"Where did you get your face painted?"

Willy pointed toward a stand at the very end of the row. There was a long line of young animals waiting their turn. At the front of the line, the face-paint artist was painting a raccoon's face to look like a tiger.

They decided not to wait in the long line. Instead, they headed off to

watch the dragonfly races. This year, dragonflies from all different parts of the forest had entered. Sophie and her friends got there just in time to see the very close finish.

Next the trio marveled at the Olsen family's apple sculpture. It was next to the Ferris wheel, right where Miss Olsen said it would be.

"Amazing!" said Sophie. The squirrels had piled at least one hundred apples into an apple tower. There were three levels—red apples on the bottom, green apples in the middle, and yellow apples on top.

"Come on!" said Sophie, scurrying off. "Let's go ride the best ride at the festival!"

Hattie and Owen hurried to catch up. "The Ferris wheel!" they shouted.

chapter 8

Don't Drop the Acorn!

Higher and higher they went! The Ferris wheel turned slowly, carrying Sophie, Hattie, and Owen all the way to the very top.

"Where did this giant wheel even come from?" Owen asked.

"Someone *found* it!" said Sophie.

"That's what I heard too!" said Hattie. "Years ago a bird spotted it at the edge of the forest. She told the festival organizers about it. A team of animals went to get it. And they made it into . . . this!"

Sophie nodded. "It's been a ride at the festival every year since."

Sophie peered over the side of their seat. She could see the whole festival! They were higher than the tops of the tents. Everyone on the ground looked like ants at an ant festival!

Sophie could just make out her mom's bake stand in the long row of stands. *That's funny,* Sophie thought. *It looks pretty empty over there.* Sophie could see lines of people at other stands, but not at Lily Mouse's. Maybe there had been long line just a minute ago? Sophie hoped so.

As they got off the Ferris wheel, the friends heard a familiar voice. "How about one more team?" the voice called.

Sophie and her friends looked over. There was Mrs. Wise, speaking

into a pinecone megaphone. "Step right up! We need one more team of three to start 'don't drop the acorn'!"

Sophie, Hattie, and Owen rushed over to say hi.

"Hello, you three!" Mrs. Wise said cheerfully.

"What kind of game is this?"
asked Sophie.

Mrs. Wise explained the rules.
"It's a relay race. One at a time, each
team member races to the flags and
back." Mrs. Wise pointed to some
flags at the far end of the grassy
area. "The fastest team wins. But

there's a twist." Mrs. Wise held up a big spoon. "Each racer has to carry along an acorn balanced in a spoon. If the acorn falls, the whole team is out."

There were already four teams at the starting line. Malcolm, the mole, and Ben and James, rabbits from school, were on one team. They waved. Sophie waved back.

Sophie, Hattie, and Owen looked at one another. "Let's do it!" cried Sophie.

"Yes!" shouted Owen and Hattie.

Mrs. Wise handed Sophie a spoon and an acorn. The three friends lined up at the start in the order they would go: Sophie first, then Hattie, then Owen.

"Ready? Set? Go!" Mrs. Wise shouted.

Sophie sprinted from the start line—then slowed way down. If she went superfast, the acorn wobbled in the spoon. *Swift but smooth,* Sophie told herself. *That's how I have to move.*

She rounded
the flag and
raced back
toward the start. Then she carefully
passed the spoon off to Hattie.

"Go, Hattie, go!" Sophie cheered.
She watched Hattie take short, grace-
ful hops. Sophie wished Hattie could
go faster. But she also didn't want her
to drop the acorn!

At last Hattie raced back and
passed the spoon to Owen. He held
it in his mouth while he slithered

toward the flag. He was going so fast!

"He's good at this!" Hattie cried.

"I know!" said Sophie. She looked over at the other teams. Two teams had dropped their acorns! Malcolm was just passing off the spoon to Ben. And the other team was way behind.

Owen was in the lead. He raced back toward Sophie and Hattie. He

crossed the finish line first!

"We did it!" Sophie called out.

Mrs. Wise hurried over. "Yes you did! Congratulations!"

She handed them their prizes— three blue ribbons, one for each of them.

"Wow!" cried Hattie as they walked away. "I've never won a festival ribbon before!"

"Me neither!" Sophie exclaimed. "Owen, you were awesome! And you won a ribbon at your very first Maple Festival!" She noticed they weren't

too far from her mom's bake stand. "You two go on without me. I want to show this to my mom!"

Sophie also kind of wanted to see if her mom needed her help. *It's sure to be busier now,* she thought as she ran along the row of stands.

Farther down the row, Sophie stopped in her tracks.

There was the bake stand. And there was her mom, alone. The festival crowds milled all around.

But no one—not one customer— was at Lily Mouse's stand.

chapter 9

Art to the
Rescue

"Mom," Sophie said as she walked up, "where is everybody?" She tucked her blue ribbon into her satchel. There were more important things to talk about.

Lily Mouse shrugged and smiled "Maybe there are just too many *other* things to see at the festival this year," she said. She ruffled the fur on Sophie's head. "It looks like we may be eating maple-apple muffins for a while."

Sophie frowned. She looked around at the other stands. "It's true," said Sophie. "There are a lot more stands this year." Everywhere she

looked, there was some-
thing to catch the eye.
There were colorful flags and
balloons. There were banners and
streamers and signs.

Was Lily Mouse's stand too hard
to find . . . in the middle of it all?

Suddenly, Sophie had an idea. "Be
right back!" she told her mom. Then
she scurried off to the edge of the
festival grounds. She snatched up
the biggest, reddest maple leaf she
could find. She carried it back to the
bake stand.

"What's that for, dear?" asked

Mrs. Mouse. But Sophie just gave her a sly smile. She pulled out a paintbrush and her paint box. Inside, she had some colors already mixed. But she needed one more. She reached into her satchel again.

She pulled out a handkerchief full of black currants. She had picked them on the way to school the other morning.

"Mom, do you have any water?" Sophie asked.

Lily Mouse nodded. She handed

Sophie a canteen she had tucked behind the stand. Sophie squashed the currants in the lid of the paint box. She added some water. Then she mixed the water and berry juice together until she got the color she wanted.

Sophie tilted the leaf up so only she could see the next part. "No peeking!" she told her mom.

After a few minutes, Sophie finally put her brush down. She held the leaf out at arm's length and studied it. Then she smiled and turned it around for her mom to see.

"Well?" Sophie said. "What do you think?"

Lily Mouse gasped.

"Sophie!" cried Lily Mouse. "It's perfect!"

"I'll say!" said George Mouse,

walking up with Winston.

"Cool sign, Sophie!" said Winston. He was holding a maple-candy lollipop.

Sophie smiled proudly. Her dad went off and found two sticks. Together, he and Sophie poked holes in either end of the leaf sign and strung it on some baker's twine that Mrs. Mouse had. They tied each end to the posts of the bake stand.

Sophie's sign fluttered high over their heads.

But will it make any difference? Sophie wondered.

chapter 10

Back in Business

At first nothing seemed to happen.

Animals walked by on their way to play games or go on the rides.

A couple of birds swooped past.

A line of ducklings led by a mother duck waddled along the row of stands. One duckling turned to gaze hungrily at Lily Mouse's treats. But his mom was moving along and he had to hurry to keep up.

Then, just as Sophie was starting to lose hope, a hummingbird zipped up. She hovered right in front of Sophie's nose. Sophie had to refocus her eyes.

"Piper!" cried Sophie, recognizing her friend from school.

Piper's mom and dad zipped up on either side of Piper.

"Thank goodness we found you!" Piper's dad said to Sophie.

"We are simply *starving* after flying around all morning!" added Piper's mom.

Piper smiled at Sophie. "We've been looking all over for your mom's bake stand," Piper said. "It's harder to find everything this year!"

The hummingbirds bought several of Lily Mouse's treats. They tasted them right then and there.

"Mmm-MMM!" said Piper's mom, trying a maple-apple muffin. "These

are the most delicious muffins I've ever tasted!"

Sophie did a happy little dance behind the bake stand. It was the first time she'd heard what someone—other than her mom—thought of her recipe.

Soon, a few more animals stopped at the bake stand. They looked at all the treats, trying to choose. Behind them, Sophie saw

other animals look up at her sign and point.

More and more animals got in line. Sophie moved to her mom's side. She handed the customers their baked goods as they ordered.

They were working quickly. But

the line was growing quickly, too!
Before Sophie knew it, the line was
winding way down the row of stands.

"Looks like we have lots of tired
and hungry customers!" Lily Mouse
whispered to Sophie.

Sophie nodded. "Ready for your

treats!" she whispered back.

"*Our* treats!" Lily Mouse said with a wink.

A bit later, Hattie and Owen came running up. They were excited to see how busy the bake stand had gotten. Sophie asked her mom if she could take a quick break. She gave her friends some treats. They sat behind the bake stand and nibbled away happily.

"Yum!" Hattie said. She was trying a waffle-cream sandwich. "This is *really* good!"

Owen agreed as he tasted a

poppy-seed dough-
nut. "Did you make
this?"

"I helped," Sophie
said proudly. "And
those recipes were
my ideas!"

Hattie and Owen were very
impressed.

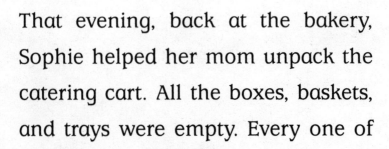

That evening, back at the bakery,
Sophie helped her mom unpack the
catering cart. All the boxes, baskets,
and trays were empty. Every one of

the treats had been sold at the festival.

"Well, Sophie," said Mrs. Mouse as she closed up the cabinets, "that was the busiest bake stand I've ever had." She pulled Sophie into a big hug. "I could not have done it without you."

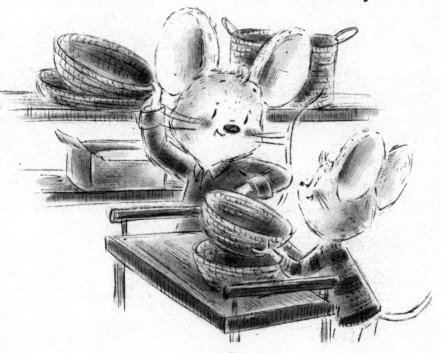

Sophie hugged her mom back. "It was really fun! Can I be your assistant again next year?" Sophie asked.

Mrs. Mouse burst out laughing. "Let's wait a few hours before we start planning for next year. Okay?"

"Okay," Sophie replied with a smile.

In the meantime, there would be a reminder of their festival success, hanging front and center in Lily Mouse's bakery.

The End

Here's a peek at the next
Adventures of Sophie Mouse book!

Sophie yawned and sat up in her bed. The early morning light glowed at her window. She squinted and blinked hard.

Sophie rubbed her eyes. She gasped. *Is that what I think it is?* she thought excitedly.

Her vision cleared. White flakes

drifted past her window. Snow! It was snowing!

Sophie leaped out of bed. She pressed her nose and whiskers against the frosty window. Outside, a blanket of white covered the sleep-ing forest.

"A snow day!" Sophie squeaked. "At last!" It was the first snowfall since winter had come. Her class at Silverlake Elementary had been on winter break for a week. But now the wintertime fun could really begin!

Still in her pajamas, Sophie tip-toed downstairs. She went to the front door and pulled it open. A little pile of snow fell onto the floor.

Sophie looked around. The forest was a glistening winter wonderland! Sophie breathed in the crisp air. Her ears perked up, listening. It was so quiet and still—except for clumps of snow softly falling from trees. Sophie imagined all the animals tucked away in their cozy homes.

"You're up early," said a voice behind her. Sophie turned. Her dad, George Mouse, was coming downstairs. "I can't imagine why," he added with a smile.